CATCH THAT RAT!

For Jess, who caught that rat - CH
To Oliver and Daniel - TM

SIMON AND SCHUSTER
First published in Great Britain in 2013 by
Simon and Schuster UK Ltd
1st Floor, 222 Gray's Inn Road, London, WC1X 8HB
A CBS Company

Text copyright © 2013 Caryl Hart
(www.carylhart.com)
Illustrations copyright © 2013 Tom McLaughlin

The rights of Caryl Hart and Tom McLaughlin to be
identified as the author and illustrator of this work
has been asserted by them in accordance with the
Copyright, Designs and Patents Act, 1988

A CIP catalogue record for this book is available from
the British Library upon request

ISBN: 978-1-84738-930-5 (HB)
ISBN: 978-1-84738-931-2 (PB)
ISBN: 978-0-85707-711-0 (ebook)
Printed in China
10 9 8 7 6 5 4 3 2 1

The inclusion of author or illustrator website addresses
in this book does not constitute an endorsement by
or an association with Simon and Schuster UK Ltd of
such sites or the content, products, advertising or other
materials presented on such sites.

CATCH THAT RAT!

Caryl Hart and Tom McLaughlin

SIMON AND SCHUSTER
London   New York   Sydney   Toronto   New Delhi

I went out this morning and what did I see?
A white-whiskered rat, looking straight back at me.

With scratchy pink claws
and a pointy pink nose,
it was dressed in some raggedy baggy old clothes.

Then, suddenly, SQUEAK! It jumped over my toes!

QUICK! CATCH THAT RAT!

It darted right in through my open front door,
then **skittered** and **scuttered** across the hall floor.

It streaked round the sofa
    where Grandmother sat.

It shot up her stockings and **leaped** on her hat.

My granny shrieked,
"Somebody FIND ME A CAT!"

QUICK!
CATCH
THAT
RAT!

"Keep still!" cried the postman. "I've got a great plan."
He emptied his sack then he dived towards Gran.
He swept the sack down over Grandmother's head . . .
but missed that white rat and caught Grandma instead!

Then straight up the chimney that little rat fled.

QUICK! CATCH THAT RAT!

I ran to my granny and helped her break free.

"Let's go!" Granny cried.

"To the roof! Follow me!"

She squeezed up the chimney and started to climb.
The postie and I followed closely behind.
It was sooty and dark but we just didn't mind!

QUICK!
CATCH
THAT
RAT!

"We'll help!" cried some builders.
"We know what to do!

We'll squish it, we'll squash it,
we'll stick it with glue."

The rat found a drain pipe
and slid to the ground.

We had to keep up,
so we followed it down.
Then it leapt on a bus
and went off towards town!

QUICK! CATCH THAT RAT!

We jumped in a cab crying, "Follow that bus!" The taxi zoomed off in a great cloud of dust.

"We're chasing that rodent," the builders explained. "It's off to the airport!" The driver exclaimed. "Look there! It's your rat, getting onto a plane."

QUICK! CATCH THAT RAT!

We bought lots of tickets and ran to get in.

The doors were all locked, so we clung to the wing.

The plane shot straight upwards and out into space,
then flew to a faraway alien place!

The **rat** scurried out
and we took up the chase.

QUICK

CATCH THAT...

"ST

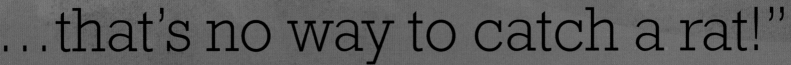

…that's no way to catch a rat!"

Right there stood an alien, scaly and red,
with **twenty-six** eyes on long stalks
round his head.

"The poor thing is frightened. She's shaking!" he said.

"Look! Poor scared rat.

You have to be gentle.

Don't scare her. Don't shout.

Just give her a biscuit

and then she'll come out."

I took out some cake crumbs and crouched in the sand.
The rat scurried closer then sat on my hand.

And everyone whispered,
"Now, isn't that grand!"

Shhhh. Poor scared rat.

I stroked the rat's fur. It was soft as can be.

"I'm calling you Pinkie. Now come home with me."

Now Pinkie looks sweet with her ears tied in bows.

I've dressed her in hand-knitted little pink clothes.

And I've painted the nails on her little pink toes.

Awww! Cute Pet Rat!

She lives in a special house under the stairs.
And **loves** having tea with my dolls and my bears.

And when Pinkie and I go outside in the sun,
my rat gets so lively, she just wants to. . .